T0194935

Judge Me Not

Beatrice Williams

WESTBOW
PRESS®
A DIVISION OF THOMAS NELSON
& ZONDERVAN

Scripture quotations marked NLT are taken from the Holy Bible, New Living
Translation, copyright 1996, 2004, 2007. Used by permission of Tyndale
House Publishers, Inc. Carol Stream, Illinois 60188. All rights reserved.

WestBow Press books may be ordered through booksellers or by contacting:

WestBow Press
A Division of Thomas Nelson & Zondervan
1663 Liberty Drive
Bloomington, IN 47403
www.westbowpress.com
1 (866) 928-1240

ISBN: 978-1-9736-1020-5 (sc)
ISBN: 978-1-9736-1019-9 (hc)
ISBN: 978-1-9736-1021-2 (e)

Library of Congress Control Number: 2017918680

Print information available on the last page.

WestBow Press rev. date: 12/14/2017

Contents

1

In 1931, on a farm four miles from a small town called Greenleaf, a baby boy named Jack was born to a white couple named Mel and Velma Wallace. Jack was the first of their three children. Three years after Jack was born, Mel and Velma had another son and named him Austin. The couple thought it would be a good idea if their sons had a baby sister to play with. Three years later, they had a baby girl, and they named her after Mel's mother, Martha. Baby Martha brought joy to the family with her vibrant personality.

Mel was a farmer and had to work very hard to support his family the best he could. Due to a lack of education, Mel and his wife, Velma, did not have much income flowing in. Velma was a housewife. When Jack was three, Mel started teaching him how to interact negatively toward people of different races. Velma did not appreciate the way Mel decided to raise his children; however, Mel was the breadwinner, so whatever he said went. From time to time, Velma would speak up about how wrong it was for him to teach their children to be racist. Often, this would lead to heated arguments and physical abuse in front of their children. The children grew to be afraid of their father. This affected Jack more than the others. Jack would intervene and attempt to stop the fights, but he would end up getting hurt in the process.

When Jack turned fourteen, he was ready to attend high school. There weren't any schools in the small town of Greenleaf, so he had to travel four towns away to go to school. Luckily for him, he had an aunt named Mabel who lived in the town of Richburn, where he planned to attend school. His aunt agreed to let him live with her on weekdays in order to make it convenient for Jack to attend school. Jack would go back home on weekends and holidays until he was through with high school. Jack attended a diverse school called Greentree High School. He had a difficult time adjusting to his new environment because he was not familiar with anyone at his school. Within a few months, Jack managed to find a couple of friends to hang out with. Soon after, Jack began getting into trouble because he started bullying other students who weren't white. Because he was raised to be a racist by his father, Jack was filled with rage and hatred for anyone who was not white.

One day while Jack was having lunch in the cafeteria with some of his friends, he spotted the most beautiful girl he had ever seen standing in the lunch line, getting her lunch.

Jack said to his friends in a very excited voice, "Hey, guys! I just saw the prettiest girl I've ever laid my eyes on."

Jack's friends all turned at the same time to see this girl who had Jack's mouth hanging past his knees and his eyes out of their sockets. Jack's friends responded, "Wow! Jack, she is gorgeous!"

Jack replied, "Yes, one day she will be my wife and the mother of my kids."

Jack's friends burst into laughter and started joking around, telling Jack that the girl would never be his wife because a girl like that would only marry him in his wildest dreams. That hurt his feelings because deep down in his heart, he wanted this girl to someday be his wife.

2

The next day, Jack arrived to school to find out that he had been relocated to another class down the hall due to overcrowding. Of course he was not happy about the change, but he resigned himself hesitantly. While Jack started walking down the hallway to his new classroom, he spotted a girl who resembled the girl from yesterday. He approached her, but to his dismay, it was not the girl of his dreams. When Jack finally got to his new classroom, there were no seats available near the front. Jack was forced to sit in the back of the class. While walking to his seat, he noticed that the only seat available was the one next to the actual girl of his dreams! As he took his seat, his heart began pounding in his chest.

The teacher said, "Jack, please come to the front of the class and introduce yourself." Reluctantly, he walked to the front of the class, turned, looked directly in the eyes of the girl of his dreams, and said, "Hi, my name is Jack."

As Jack returned to his seat, the pretty girl turned to Jack and said, "Hi, my name is Caroline Van-Patrick." Jack smiled as he and Caroline began to shake each other's hands. It wasn't long after that introduction that Jack and Caroline became friends. They helped one another with homework and hung out all the time. A dilemma began. Jack's friends were not happy about Jack's newfound relationship. In fact, they were a little jealous.

Jack and Caroline officially started dating and continued to date throughout high school. At this time, they were both seniors and getting ready to graduate. Jack was nervous about graduation because he had goofed off and was not getting passing grades in his classes. He was not sure if he was going to graduate. Fortunately for him, he received good news that he would. Caroline was heading off to college in the middle of August, and Jack was going to join the service at the end of July. They knew they did not have much time to spend with one another, so after graduation, Jack and Caroline spent the entire summer together. And when they said their goodbyes, they made a promise to forever be in love.

3

Jack and Caroline kept in touch until he moved to another unit after his basic training. While Jack was in the service, he suffered many injuries, but none of them were too serious.

Four years passed, and it was almost time for him to leave the service. Unfortunately, at that time, his unit was sent to war. While in combat, a bullet grazed his arm and knee, making it impossible for him use them. He was forced to relearn how to use them again.

Released from duty, Jack headed back home to Greenleaf. When he returned, he learned that Caroline had graduated college with her bachelor's in sociology and moved to the town in which he lived. After being in town for a little over a week, Jack was finally able to meet up with Caroline. Jack could not believe how beautiful she had grown, and Caroline could not believe how handsome he had gotten since his departure. Jack and Caroline started dating again, but this time he knew he never wanted to be separated from her again. He improved himself by getting a job so he could save up enough money to marry Caroline. Jack got a job at Beatrice's Steel Factory. Even though he suffered from injuries, he was able to work productively. Jack was a hard worker and dependable, so when Jack's manager decided to retire, he recommended Jack for the position. With enthusiasm, Jack accepted the position.

It was Valentine's Day, and Jack proposed to Caroline. A year later, they got married. The ceremony was everything they had hoped it would be and more. A year after their marriage, the Wallaces brought their first son into the world, Jeff. When Jeff was two years old, their second son, named Sam, arrived. Jack continued working at the factory while Caroline was a social worker for the local Department of Children and Families, both doing whatever it took to provide a happy home for Jeff and Sam.

4

Over the years, Jack began exhibiting racist behaviors. One by one, he fired all employees who were not Caucasian. One day out of the clear blue, Jack received a phone call from Vince, his former employer. Vince told Jack that he had heard about the dismissal of employees down at the factory. Jack did not respond to whether the accusations were true or not. He simply replied, "Vince, mind your business! I am the factory manager now, and I did what was right for the factory."

Upset by what he had heard, Vince told Jack that he had made a huge mistake by firing those employees on account of them being a different race. Jack responded by telling Vince that their race had nothing to do with them being fired; it was the fact that none of them were pulling their weight at the factory. Vince, disappointed in Jack's actions, told him that he should have never recommended him for the position as manager. Jack replied by telling Vince that he should get over his disappointment. Vince, very upset by the conversation, ended by telling Jack that he was a wicked man and that he was going to get him one day. Jack felt threatened, so he called his friend Randy to meet up with him at the local bar to talk about his conversation with Vince. Upon his arrival at the bar, Jack saw an African American man kissing a Caucasian woman.

Already filled with rage from what happened between him and Vince, Jack shouted to the couple, "You cannot go anywhere nowadays without seeing these monkey guys with their hands around our white women! They need to go back to their country where they belong!" Meanwhile, Randy was sitting at the bar having drinks and waiting for Jack to walk in.

Jack finally met up with Randy and began to tell him about the conversation with Vince. When Jack finished the story, Randy replied, "Why is Vince worrying about what is going on in the factory, anyway? He is retired. He should be out playing golf and not worrying about those Hispanic and black workers. They should have never come to this country."

After an hour and a half of drinking and talking, Jack and Vince began speaking louder and more ruthlessly. They were drunk and careless about what they said and who was around. They were shouting out racist comments about other customers in the bar. Many of the customers were very disturbed and began complaining to the bartender. The bartender reported the complaints to his manager, and the manager was forced to ask Jack and Vince to leave. The two drunken friends refused to leave because they felt they were loyal customers of the bar. The manager called the police and had them escorted out.

5

C aroline had to go grocery shopping to pick up a few things for dinner that night. While at the store, she ran into her friend Vernice. A conversation sparked, and during that conversation, Vernice mentioned that it was a shame that Caroline's husband had fired all the African American and Hispanic employees at the factory.

Caroline, unclear of what she was talking about, kindly asked, "What's an awful shame? What did my husband do?"

Realizing that Caroline did not know of the incident, Vernice said, "You mean you didn't know, Caroline?"

"Didn't know what?" Caroline responded.

Vernice replied, "You didn't know that Jack fired all the Hispanic and black employees shortly after he became manager?"

Caroline just stood there with a dazed look on her face, shrugged her shoulders, and shook her head.

Amazed that Jack would do such a thing and unable to grasp what her husband had done, Caroline furiously rushed home to confront him. As she was pulling up in the driveway, Jack pulled up at the same time. Jack got out to help Caroline. She could smell the alcohol on him.

Caroline yelled, "Jack Wallace! Have you been drinking?" Jack answered by telling Caroline that he had only had a few drinks. She did not believe him because he could barely stand on his own two feet. She grabbed his hand and took him inside so he would not fall over. Then she went back outside to get the groceries. Upon her return, she found Jack stumbling over the furniture. Right there and then, she knew it was not a good time to talk to him about what she had heard. The next morning after breakfast, Caroline told Jack that she needed to talk to him. Jack agreed but did not know what the conversation would be about.

From the tone of Caroline's voice, Jack knew it was something serious. He stated, "Honey, is something wrong?"

Caroline responded "Yes! Seriously wrong!" Caroline proceeded by saying that when she had gone to the grocery store the day before, she'd run into one of her friends, and this friend had told her what he'd done to everyone but the Caucasians down at the factory. Jack was not sorry for what he did, but he did not like his wife being angry with him. He decided it was best for him to remain silent.

Caroline could not stand the silence. "Is that true or not?" Caroline asked.

"Yes, that's true. I did what I had to do," Jack responded.

She proceeded to ask him, "Why did you feel that you had to fire only the blacks and Hispanics?"

Jack said, "Well, most of them weren't good workers, as everyone thought they were, and they were just looking for a free ride. I don't believe in free rides."

Caroline replied, "Jack, how could you do that? You don't even know if they had families. Were you concerned about that at all?"

Curtly, Jack said, "I am not concerned about them or their families. I am only concerned about how my wife is turning against me for some Hispanics and blacks!"

Caroline said, "I am not turning against you. I'm just upset with what you did and why you did it." After a brief moment of silence, Caroline commented, "What if someone did that to you? How would you feel?"

Jack answered by saying that it would never happen to him because he was neither black nor Hispanic. He proceeded to say that he no longer wanted to talk about the situation.

Caroline was not raised to hate people because they were of a different skin color. She knew Jack was a bit prejudiced in high school, but she'd thought he would grow out of it. Unfortunately, it had gotten worse over the years. She warned Jack that the people he fired may seek revenge on him or even harm him. Jack stated that he was not worried and that they were beneath him. Caroline responded by saying, "Jack, you are absolutely incorrect! We were all created equal, which means that you are no better than they are."

Jack, upset by what Caroline had said, pulled back his right arm and slapped her across her face. Caroline fell to the floor and began crying. She could not believe what her husband had just done; neither could Jack. Jack kneeled down to the floor next to Caroline and said, "Honey, I'm sorry. Please forgive me. You know I would never hurt you." Caroline stared at him with tears streaming down her face. She started to get off the floor and looked out the corner of her eye to see their son Jeff coming down the stairs from his room.

He yelled, "Dad! What did you do to Mom?" His dad told him to go back upstairs to his room.

Jeff replied, "No! I will not leave until I know she is all right." He proceeded to ask his father, "Did you hit her?"

Jack replied, "We were just talking. It got out of hand."

Jeff screamed, "You're a monster!" as he helped his mother up to sit on a chair at the kitchen table. Caroline reassured Jeff that she was all right and that he should go back upstairs with no worries. Although he did not like the idea of leaving his mother downstairs, he listened and went upstairs. When he reached the top of the stairs, he ran to his brother Sam's room. He told Sam that he heard a loud noise downstairs earlier and assumed his mom had broken a dish or something. To his dismay, he found their mother on the floor with their father hovering over her. He did not understand why their father was so hotheaded and felt as if their father had no right to ever put his hands on their mother. As Jeff was speaking, Sam was curious as to what they were arguing about. Jeff did not know, but he'd heard that his father had fired all of the blacks and Hispanics at the factory.

Sam asked, "Why?"

Jeff responded, "I don't know, but I know it had something to do with them not being white." He added, "I do not know why Dad is so racist because if it weren't for a black man, he would not be alive today."

Unsure of what Jeff was saying, Sam asked, "What do you mean?" Jeff continued by saying that when their father was in the service and went to war, a black man saved their father's life by intercepting a bullet for him. Based on the dazed look on Sam's face, it was clear he'd never known that.

He asked Jeff how he knew about the story, and Jeff responded, "No one knows about this. See, one of Dad's old army buddies slipped and told me at the barbeque we went to two months ago. He told me not to mention it because Dad did not want anyone to know. Shoot! I don't even think Mom knows, so we'd better not mention it."

Caroline came upstairs to see if Jeff was all right because he seemed upset when she told him to go upstairs earlier. She asked him if he was okay, and Jeff said he was fine, but he wanted to know where his father was. His father was on the front porch with one of his friends who had paid him a visit.

Sam asked, "Why was Dad so mad? He is a monster! Why did he hit you?"

Caroline said, "No, boys! Your father is not a monster, and he loves us very much, but sometimes he just loses his temper. Things are just more complicated than they seem. Okay, honey?"

"I do not care about what's so complicated, just as long as he never hits you again," Sam replied.

Caroline gave him a hug, and while doing that, she began to explain to her sons that their father was raised by their grandpa. During the explanation, Jeff blurted, "Was Grandpa Mel racist too?" Surprised by what her son said, she tried to change the subject. She never discussed anything about racism with the children, so where could they possibly have found out about it? She asked her sons how school went yesterday, but Jeff was still waiting on the answer to his question. She answered him by saying their grandfather raised their father to not associate with people who were not the same color as he was. She swore that was not the way her sons were going to be raised.

At that moment, Jack came back into the house and went upstairs. That is when he heard Caroline talking to the boys. He did not hear everything, but he heard enough. Jack went back downstairs and called Caroline to come down. The boys begged their mother not to go, and she told them that everything was all right now. Then, she went downstairs. Jack told Caroline that he had heard some of her conversation and did not appreciate her trying to turn his sons against him. Caroline exclaimed, "Your sons! I think you mean our sons!" Then Caroline went on to say that she was pretty sure he was not the one who had carried them for nine months each. Jack said that if he did not want his family to socialize with people he thinks are beneath them, then that was just the way it was going to be. She exclaimed, "If that is the way you want to live your life, it is your own choice, but I am not going to let you influence me or our sons to live like you."

Jack was so upset by the way Caroline was standing up to him, but this time he could not do or say anything. Caroline told Jack that she loved him but hoped one day he would change his evil ways. He responded by saying, "Sure! Whatever!"

6

The Williams

William (Willie) and Shannon Robinson had just moved to Greenleaf. They'd met nine years ago at a local Laundromat. From there, they'd begun dating and decided to marry at an early age. After marriage, the couple decided not to have any children. Life was hard for both Willie and Shannon. Both of them had only a high school education, and they lived with Willie's parents. While going to school to become a nursing assistant, Shannon had a job at the local supermarket. Soon after that, she graduated at the top of her class and began working at a nursing home.

Finally, Willie and Shannon were able to afford an apartment of their own. Living in a one-bedroom apartment, the Robinson decided this would be a perfect time to start a family. After about six months of trying, Shannon finally got pregnant with their first child. One day, Shannon thought that maybe she would go back to school to become a registered nurse. She decided that she would talk to Willie about her decision. Willie did not like the idea of her being pregnant while attending school. He tried to explain to her that the timing was not right. "Honey, I understand that you want to better our lives, but having all that stress is dangerous for you and the baby," said Willie. Shannon was determined to become a registered nurse, so that next Monday morning, she went and registered at a community college. While in line, Shannon overheard some white students making racist comments, but she stayed strong and continued to wait in line to register.

A couple weeks went by, and Shannon delivered a beautiful baby boy. They named him Martin. Life seemed to be going great for the Robinsons. While Shannon was at school and Willie at work, Willie's parents watched Martin; and at night, Willie and Shannon would be with their son. After a year, Shannon finally graduated from the nursing program. She got a job at Mary Joseph Memorial Hospital as a registered nurse. Even though Willie was still working as a mechanic, he had dreams of owning his own mechanic shop. He felt that would have to be placed on hold because Shannon was expecting again. Now that the family was becoming even bigger, the Robinsons decided to purchase a house. Since they were saving up, they decided to buy a home in a nice neighborhood. They visited a real estate agent, and they came across a beautiful three-bedroom home with two bathrooms in Greenleaf. This was going to be a big move and transition for them, but they felt it was well worth it.

Life got better for the Robinsons. They had a set schedule where Shannon would get the children ready for school before her morning shift at the hospital, Willie would bring them to school, and Shannon would head off to work for the day. When she came home, she would prepare dinner and get the children ready for bed. If they needed help with homework, she was there to help. It was clear that she loved her family and would do anything for them to stay safe.

Most of the residents in the town were Caucasian. The blacks, Hispanics, and certain Jews had a hard time living in the town. There was a group of racist people making their lives miserable. It seemed as if they were trying to run them out of the neighborhood, but they stood strong and did not let the hostility ruin them. Soon after the Robinsons moved in, people began burning crosses in front of the Robinsons' house.

One day, when there was a group of racist Caucasians standing near the Robinsons' house, Shannon walked outside. As they stared at her, she said, "I am a lovely and strong black woman who does not ask for trouble from anyone. Whoever dislikes me and my family and judges us based on our skin color has no right. Only my creator can judge me. My husband and I work so hard to provide for our family. We are trying to give them a better life. We teach them right from wrong, and take them to school and church. We will be welcomed in this neighborhood because we paid to live in this neighborhood."

She peeked over to the ground and found a hate letter. She bought it over to Willie, and he shouted, "I am taking this to the authorities!"

They went to the police station and showed them the hate letter and told them about the burning cross in front of their home. The police made no effort to help them. All they could say was that if nobody was hurt, then there was nothing they could do.

"So, we gotta wait until someone is hurt or dead before you do something," Willie said.

"What about us? We are important citizens in the neighborhood too," Shannon exclaimed.

Willie agreed. "Right! We pay taxes just like they do. We want equal protection and justice."

Shannon stated, "The police talk to us as though we do not exist, but in the eyes of the Lord, we do."

7

Acouple years passed, and Martin was now seventeen, Alicia fifteen, and the youngest, Marvin, was six. Willie and Shannon were anxious and afraid of the racism going on in the town. For a long time, Shannon would beg Willie to move because the neighborhood that she once viewed as beautiful was now one of the most racist neighborhoods to live in. Willie would not leave. He believed that they were human beings like everyone else and that they too had rights. He would say, "I am an American, and I refuse to let the white man drive me and my family out of the house I worked for all my life."

One early morning, Willie and the kids were on their way out. Jack and his friends drove by Willie's house and shouted, "Get out of our neighborhood! I promise I'll kill ya and ya family if you don't leave."

Although he was upset, Willie did not do or say anything to Jack or his friends. He remained quiet out of respect for his kids. When Willie arrived at the school, he held his kids' hands, kneeled in front of them, and said, "Not all white people are like that. There are some really good white people out there in the world. Okay?"

"Okay," his kids replied in unison. When Willie saw his daughter crying, his heart broke in two, and he vowed that his kids would never go through this again. Alicia looked at her father and asked him to explain why that white man was so mean and angry.

Willie said, "Because, baby, people like him don't like people who are not the same color."

Just then, Martin put his arm around his little sister's neck and said, "Alicia, everything is going to be all right." Alicia laid her head on Martin's shoulder, and he continued to tell her, "Don't cry. They only hate us because we are strong, beautiful people. What is important is God's love for us." Willie stopped the kids and began to have a little talk with them.

He told them, "Don't let anyone tell you that you're not worth living. Only you can determine your success. All you have to do is work hard on your goals, and don't forget to always help others. I don't care who they are. Most of all, don't be prejudiced against anyone because, at the end of your life, you have to answer to God for all your actions." Willie concluded by saying that white people were not the only people who were prejudiced. "There are black people who are racist, as well as Hispanic people. You all have the right to live. I may not be a rich man or give you the world, but your mother and I can give you love and teach you to respect yourselves and others. Do not be judgmental toward anyone who is different from you."

Willie's wife and his kids were all he had to live for, and he wanted to make sure his kids knew that family and God should always come first in their lives. Willie vowed that even though he could not stop prejudice, he would do his best to protect his children from people like Jack Wallace.

One Sunday morning, Willie decided to take his family to the local restaurant. Upon their arrival, they had to wait to be seated, but no one came. They asked for help, but of course, everyone around them was being seated.

Shortly after, Willie was annoyed and said to the hostess, "Excuse me, but my family has been waiting to be seated and everyone else has been seated except for us."

The hostess called the owner over, and he asked, "Do we have a problem here?"

Willie replied, "Yes!" He then began to explain the situation, and as he was explaining, the owner cut him off and said, "Well I am sorry, but we no longer have tables available. Besides, breakfast is over."

Willie asked, "What do you mean there is no table available? There are three tables empty, and those people who just sat down are being served breakfast."

In response, the owner said, "If I say there is no table, then there is no table. This is my restaurant! I know you black people love to make a scene. Don't make a scene and just git!"

Willie looked at Shannon, and Shannon looked at her kids. They took them all by the hands and led them outside to get in the car, feeling hurt and defeated. Meanwhile, Willie stayed inside the restaurant, and he stared the owner in his eyes. He said, "I too was born in the USA, and I too have rights in this country. You might not like me, but you will respect me and my family." Then he walked out feeling as if he had a rock lifted off his chest.

Willie got in the car with a huge smile on his face and began to drive home.

Shannon asked, "Baby, what happened?" and Willie said, "Baby, I got a little bit of my dignity back." Shannon looked at her husband and her three children. She smiled with content because she knew everything was going to be all right.

One hot weekend in the summer, Martin and Sam were playing a game of basketball on the street in front of their house. Suddenly, they got into an argument. The two boys got into a fight with each other. Then Ms. Albury, the boys' neighbor, ran into her house and called the police. The police arrived and arrested Sam and Martin and took them to the county jail to be booked. Sergeant Ron called their parents to let them know and to alert them that they would be staying overnight. The next morning, Caroline rushed to the jailhouse to pick up Sam and take him home. On the car ride home, Caroline asked Sam what the fight was all about. Then she told Sam that he should know not to get into fights.

Meanwhile, back at the jailhouse, Martin's father, Willie, approached the cashier to pay for Martin's release. The receptionist informed Willie that Martin's bail had been denied. Willie said, "You denied my son's bail? Why? Am I not allowed to take my son home?" Sergeant Ron approached and explained that they were not finished with booking Martin because he was being charged with juvenile delinquency. Willie told Sergeant Ron that his child has never been arrested. Then he realized that someone was missing.

"Wait," he said. "Where is the boy that my son was fighting?"

The sergeant said, "Sam? He has been released."

Willie got upset and exclaimed, "So you guys think that's fair? You released one boy and not the other?" He continued, "The other guy couldn't have been no Negro. He gotta be white because I know that would be the only reason why you would release him." He paused for a brief moment and then said, "If I can't take my son home, can I at least see him?"

Sergeant Ron told Willie that visiting hours were over and that he would have to come back in the morning. This outraged Willie even more.

"I'm not leaving until I see my son! What is it that black people have to do to get justice in this country? How dare you keep an innocent person because of the color of his skin! That is my flesh and blood behind those bars, and if you don't let him go by tomorrow morning, I'm going to call the NAACP, and we will get my son out one way or the other," Willie shouted. Willie turned around and began to leave when Officer Kelly walked in and notice that Willie was crying.

Officer Kelly asked, "Sir! Why are you crying?"

Willie said, "Officer, they're refusing to let my son come home with me."

"What did he do?" Officer Kelly asked.

"He was in a street fight with a white boy. Sergeant whatever his name is released the white boy and kept my son in jail," said Willie.

Officer Kelly said to Willie, "Don't you worry about a thing. I'm going to get your son out of here."

As Sergeant Ron was processing the records, Officer Kelly walked over to him and said, "Two kids got into a fight; you only release one, and that one kid happens to be white? They are equally responsible, so both kids, black or white, should both be released. Besides, fighting is not a chargeable crime. If you are going to charge them, you are going to charge them equally." He asked for the boy to be released to his father right away. "And if he does this again, he will report him to the highest authority."

Willie watched the entire event unfold right in front of his eyes. Officer Kelly walked over to him and said, "Mr. William, do not worry. Your son is being released right now."

A tear flowed down Willie's cheek, and he said, "Thank you, Officer Kelly, for giving me my son back and for giving us the opportunity to be treated equally. God is going to bless you." Martin turned around and said thank you to the officer and walked out with his father.

When Martin reached home, his mother was so happy to see him that she started kissing him all over his face. Then, his little brother and sister joined in on the embrace. Following this, Willie decided to have a family meeting to explain the differences between right and wrong.

Jack found out what happened the next day. He was so upset and angry that the black boy was fighting with his son and was released from jail. He forced Sam to get in the car to show him who he was fighting with. "When that last light in the neighborhood goes out, Imma teach that boy a lesson," Jack said. Sam refused to get in the car after hearing that.

"No, Daddy. I don't wanna hurt anybody. He is a boy just like me. I have no resentment toward him, so why should you?" Sam pleaded.

"Quiet, boy! No boy puts his hands on my son, and since he did, he's gonna deal with me," Jack replied.

Sam replied, "If you hurt that boy, Dad, I will never forgive you. Mom did not raise me to hurt people." He thought to himself for a moment and then said, "I doubt the boy's father is reacting the way you are. Why are you so hateful? I never want to be like you."

Jack did not listen to his son. He began yelling at him, "You listen to me, and you listen to me good. I don't care what you and ya momma think or do. You kids are brainwashed by ya momma. You are white, and us whites gonna stick together. I will never stop fighting for my race."

Sam was picked up and brought to the car. His father drove off with him and told him to point out the boy. He did. Upon his arrival home, he was scared that his father would do something bad to the boy, so he told his mother. Caroline reassured her son by telling him that she would take care of his father and his plans. She waited until

Jack got home. When he did, she shouted, "If you plan to hurt the boy, I'll have no choice but to call the police."

Jack replied, "Go call the police. Do you think that will stop me?" He walked out and got into his car and drove off.

It was eight o'clock, and Martin had just come from a basketball game. He was walking home alone. He noticed a white Jeep pass him and make a U-turn through the alley across from him. Then it stopped in front of him. A man got out from the car, yelling at him, and started punching him.

He was shouting, "This is for my son! You will never do that again, boy!" He pushed Martin to the ground and said, "I hope I don't see ya again." Then he began laughing.

Martin, trying to gasp for air, stood up and said to the man, "I am not afraid of you. You could beat me up and call me all the names you want. I am a proud black man, and I am not ashamed of it. I plan to stay in this town, you racist pig!"

The man jumped into his car, stared at him, and said, "I will be back for you and ya family." He drove off.

Someone was standing outside of their house and saw everything. This person called the police. Soon, the police and ambulance arrived to take Martin to the hospital. Upon his arrival at the hospital, they called his parents. Shannon was an employee of the hospital. When Willie and Shannon arrived, no one was able to give them their son's condition, so they were forced to sit and wait it out. It was starting to get late. Night turned to day, and Willie and Shannon were told to go home and that they would be called if anything changed with Martin. Later that day, the doctors released Martin. Willie decided to have lunch with his family.

While they were at Bee's Brunch and Munch, Martin explained everything to his parents. As Martin was talking, Willie recognized a familiar face walking in. He shouted, "Hey! I know you. You're one of Jack Wallace's friends." He walked over to him and said, "Tell Jack that I saw him passing by my house in his white Jeep, and the next time his racist behind passes by my house, aggravating my family, it won't be good. Trust me! My family is my life, and I will die to protect them." He walked away with a satisfied grin on his face and returned to have lunch with his family. No one asked what he said; they were just happy to be together and well as a family.

Willie decided to pursue a case against Jack although he had no other evidence other than the anonymous witness who called the police and the ambulance for his son.

8

Officer Kelly

Officer Kelly was determined to find justice for Martin. It upset him that the chief did not want to sign the case over to him. Officer Kelly knew that Jack Wallace was the one who beat the young man, and he tried to talk some sense into the chief on how it was Jack who did the beating.

The chief said, "To make you happy, I will have a talk with Jack."

Kelly replied, "I don't want you to have a talk with Jack. I want you to arrest him." The chief walked out of his office. "You know he is guilty. Why are you protecting him?" yelled Officer Kelly as the chief left the building.

The chief arrived at Jack's house to question him about the incident in which the boy was brutally beaten on the sidewalk. He knocked, and Jack came to the door.

"Can I help you?" Jack said.

The chief replied, "Good morning, Mr. Wallace. I wanted to ask you a couple questions about a beating that happened a few days ago."

"I don't know anything about that, Chief. I was out with my friends that night. We were having a couple of drinks," responded Jack.

The chief responded, "Are you sure? As I recall, the young man involved had a fight with your son."

Jack commented, "I guess he got what he deserved, and if you don't believe me, feel free to go ask my friends, Sam, and the other men."

"If I find out you have something to do with this beating, I will be back for you," commented the chief. He walked to his car, got in, rolled the windows down, and yelled, "I will get in touch with you soon." That was the last time Jack heard from the chief.

As soon as the chief arrived at the station, he saw Officer Kelly sitting on the steps.

Kelly saw the chief, hopped up, and questioned, "What happened? Where is Jack? Why didn't you arrest him?"

The chief said, "I can't arrest him. He has an alibi. He claims to have been out with his friends, having a few drinks."

"Oh, bologna, Chief," Officer Kelly interrupted. "You know he is lying, and his friends will lie for him too. They're all racist, just like him. I cannot believe he is getting away with this. We are police officers; we are supposed to do the right thing."

The next day, a female detective named Kate Johnson transferred from another precinct to theirs. Chief O'Neil was showing her around. He introduced her to the staff. To start, he gave her a box filled with unsolved cases. As she was going through the box, there was a file that caught her eye. She pulled it out and began reading it. When she finished, she approached Officer Kelly and asked him why the case was not solved. To her, it was such a simple case along with a suspect.

Officer Kelly said, "I felt the same way. However, it is not that simple. It may be more complicated than it looks."

Officer Johnson replied, "What could be so complicated about this?"

Officer Kelly explained, "Well, Jack is one the most racist men in town, and the victim is a seventeen-year-old male who got into a fight with his son. I assume he beat him, and then the poor kid was hospitalized."

She pondered why the chief did not do anything and mentioned, "Since the chief did not do anything, is it safe to say that he is racist too?"

He replied, "I have no idea if he is or not. It is something to consider since he let someone get away with the crime."

Kate walked away and into Chief O'Neil's office. She questioned why there was nothing done about the case. "Why wasn't this racist man in jail?" she asked.

"Who told you he is a racist man?" blurted the chief. "Please don't get yourself involved with things that don't concern you," he added.

"It does not matter how I know about it. I came to you as an officer, asking you for this case, Chief," exclaimed Kate.

"Absolutely not," the chief yelled. "You have plenty of other cases you could worry about, and besides, you are new here. You do not know your way around this town."

Kate replied, "I want this case. What is so important about that guy? And what about this little boy? He deserves justice too. I will take my chances. We took an oath to serve and protect, regardless of race, and that is exactly what I am going to do."

The chief interrupted, "I guess this case is yours, but I must give you a partner to show you around the town."

The chief stepped out of his office and called in Officer Kelly. He decided to change his mind and let Officer Kelly take charge of the case as Detective Kate assists. He expected a full report by the end of the day.

The first thing Detective Kate and Officer Kelly decided to do was to go to the Williams' home to question Martin and his family in order to get information about the incident and see if Martin could identify his attacker. When they arrived there, Detective Kate introduced herself and Officer Kelly, and they began the questioning.

Martin begin to tell the detective, "All I know is that I was on my way home from a basketball game. A white Jeep stopped in front of me and a man jumped out of his car and started beating me up while calling me names." He described him as a white man, six foot tall, blue eyes, brown hair, and a low beard. "His son goes to school with me," he said.

"So, you know who he is?" Kate asked.

"I know his name and his face," replied Martin.

Kate said, "Do not worry; we will bring him to justice." She walked away and said, "I will see you soon."

Since she was new in this town, she went undercover to obtain more information about Jack, but no one was willing to talk. It seemed as though he had power over other people. As Kate approached a bar in the town, a woman in an alley called out to her. She asked Kate if she was a detective, and Kate replied, "Yes, and you are?"

She replied, "My name is Mary-Ann. I witnessed the boy getting beat up the other day. I did not want to say anything because I did not think the police would listen."

"Why is that?" Kate questioned.

"Specifically because I am black, and he is black too. Nearly all the white people in this town are racist, including some of the police officers," she responded.

"Not all white police officers are racist. All I want to know is, are you willing to testify against the person who did the beating?" Kate asked.

Mary-Ann agreed to testify and told her it was Jack. Kate thanked her and gave her a contact card just in case she needed to talk to her.

Kate and Kelly went back to the office to give the chief a report. They had substantial information to arrest Jack, including a testimony from the boy and an eyewitness willing to take the stand. They planned to call the judge to get a warrant for the arrest of Jack Wallace. The chief alerted them that the judge had taken a week off and that they would have to wait until he came back. They agreed to wait until Tuesday morning to obtain a warrant for Jack's arrest.

9

The Lopez Family

Maria Lopez had moved to Greenleaf three years ago as a single parent of two. Her husband had left her four years ago, and she'd had a hard time adjusting following that. With no trace of her husband, not even a check sent for their children, she had to provide for her family the best way she could.

At first, she was doing well with her part-time job, but since her children were getting older and needed more things, she went on the search for a second job. It was difficult to find a job in the beginning, but eventually, she found work at a nursing home as a full-time housekeeper along with a part-time night job at the local diner. Her son was fourteen when his father left them, and from there, he began acting up; moreover, he was confused. He was angry at his father for abandoning his family, and as the man of the house, he wanted to drop out of school to find a job. Maria did not have enough time to spend quality time with him, so she did not know what was going on with her son. As the mother and father, she made it a habit to always call and check up on her kids, make sure they were home, and make sure they had done their schoolwork. One night, she decided to have a talk with her son before heading off to work.

She stared at him for a while, and then he blurted out, "I am worried about you, Mom. You work too hard, and you are tired. So, I want to leave school to help you out."

She said, "I love you so much. There is only one thing I need for you to do for me. I need you to stay in school. You are intelligent, so don't throw your life away."

Edward listened to his mother and promised her that he would stay in school and graduate. Since he loved his mother and his sister, he wanted to do anything to make them happy.

Edward graduated from high school at nineteen but did not have college in mind. He decided to put college on hold for the moment. He went looking for a job at the Beatrice Steel Factory, but the manager, Jack Wallace, did not hire Hispanics or African Americans. He was not even given a chance to fill out an application, but that did not stop him. Upon his search for a new job, he found one at an elementary school as a Hispanic teacher's aide. He loved the new job. With this, he knew exactly what he wanted to do when he went to college. Since the pay was good at the school, he told his mom to leave her night job; he would be helping her with some of her bills. He could now say he was the man of the house.

It was Sarah Lopez's last year in high school, and she planned to go college, as her brother aspired for her. Her main goal was to get scholarships to help pay for her school because she knew her mother would not be able to afford it. Unfortunately, the racism in and around the world would be a minor bump in the road to her goal.

So she studied night and day in order to write an amazing essay to win this scholarship.

They told her that her essay was amazing; however, another student was more qualified to get the scholarship. Sam Wallace, a young, Caucasian, C-average student won the scholarship. Needless to say, this upset her. She worked hard to maintain an A-average, and to see someone who barely tried win the scholarship confused her. It could have been the cruel, prejudiced mentality of society or it may have been that she really was not qualified. No one knew, nor did they ever find out. Though she was disappointed, her family did not want her to worry. They wanted to make sure, somehow, that her tuition for college got paid.

To get rid of the disappointment, Maria took the kids out for lunch. As they all sat there in silence, waiting to be seated, Maria said, "People can be cruel sometimes but do not let that stop you from achieving your dreams. Since you are young, you have a long life ahead of you. So, never stop fighting that good fight; never stop fighting for what you believe in."

Sarah did not want the whole lunch to be about her, so she changed the subject. "Enough about me," she said. "What about you, Edward? What is going on in your life? All you do is work hard to take care of us. I want you to get out and have some fun. Maybe find yourself a nice girlfriend."

He replied, "Well, do not worry, little sister. I have a girlfriend already. Her name is Lisa." While gazing out the window, he continued, "She is a wonderful, beautiful, kind-hearted, white woman. I am pretty sure you guys would love her."

Sarah asked, "If she is so wonderful, why haven't we met her yet? How did you two meet, anyway?"

With a look of adoration, he said, "We met in the strangest way. It is kind of funny, actually. On my way home from work, I saw this beautiful woman on the side of road, standing and walking around her car. I walked over to her and tried to help her out. I couldn't fix the car, though. Then I asked her if she had anyone she could call to help her. She said no. I offered to take her home. She said no again."

He laughed and continued, "Stubborn little one. She told me it was not a good idea. Since she did not want me to help, I asked her what she was going to do. She took a few minutes to walk around and think, I suppose, and she changed her mind. She wanted to know if it was okay for me to drop her halfway."

"Halfway," his sister interrupted.

With a quick glance, he said, "I asked her if it was because she had a boyfriend, and she said no. From there, I understood why halfway. But halfway was better than no way at all. We drove in silence, and as she told me where to drop her, I reluctantly asked her to go out with me. She did not respond, and then she turned to look at me and said that I seemed like a nice young man, but I would not want to be involved with her. She said, 'Right now in my life, things are complicated. I would not expect you to understand. My family is racist. Basically, they are prejudiced against everyone who is not white. If they find out I am with you, they may kill you and me. I do not want anything to happen to you on account of me.' I asked if she was racist, and she said no. I was infatuated."

Sarah looked at her brother and said, "She sounds like a wonderful person, but if she says her parents are racist, you gotta be careful. Please! I just want you to be happy, and I do not want you to get hurt."

Lisa was the only child of Bo and Lauriane Clark. At nineteen, she was still living under her parents' strict guidance. Lisa wanted to become an artist and did not believe there was a future for her in this town. She was not happy here, and the only time she was, was when she was with her boyfriend, Edward. Lisa and Edward had been secretly dating for some time. She had not even told her best friend, Adrianne, with whom she shared everything, that she had a boyfriend. She was in love with him but could not bring him home because he was Hispanic. It hurt her to have to leave their relationship a secret, but it made her so happy to be able to share her love with someone other than Adrianne. Today, she decided to tell her best friend about Edward. She approached her at school, pulled her to the side of the cafeteria, and said, "I met someone five months ago, and now I am in love with him. His name was Edward Lopez and I wanted to tell you about him, but I was afraid."

Adrianne said, "What are you afraid of? How could you not tell me?"

She replied, "Because I was afraid you would not agree because he is not white."

Adrianne responded, "Well, I am so happy for you. So, when will I meet this wonderful man of yours?"

She said, "Soon, but not now. I need you to promise me that you will not go around telling everyone. You know how people are in this town, especially my parents." Adrianne agreed not to tell anyone; however, she had an ugly trait that Lisa did not know about. Adrianne became jealous. Lisa was happy and did not spend time with her anymore. They barely saw each other.

One day, Adrianne got into an argument with her boyfriend, Mike, and she said to him, "You treat me as if I'm not special. Why can't you treat me like Lisa's boyfriend treats her? I wish was with someone like Edward."

Mike, bewildered, said, "That Puerto Rican Edward? I did not know she was with him or that she had a boyfriend at all. Does her daddy know?"

She replied, "No. Don't say anything to her parents or anyone else. They have no idea."

"Why not?" he said. "I am going to tell. I hate those people."

Adrianne pleaded. Lisa would know that she was one that told him.

One evening, Adrianne's boyfriend Mike passed by Lisa's house. He saw Bo, Lisa's father, outside, watering his grass. He stopped to say hi and strike up a conversation. He said, "Did you know that your daughter is going out with a Hispanic man, Bo?"

Bo replied with confusion. "You are lying, boy."

Mike said, "Ask her." Bo angrily ran into the house and opened his desk. He picked up a shotgun. He ran through the house, shouting, "I'm gonna kill 'em! I'm gonna kill 'em!" He called his daughter downstairs. When she came down, her dad began yelling, "I heard you been seeing a Hispanic boy. Tell me it ain't true, Lisa."

She looked at her dad and said, "Yes. I have been seeing him for five months, and I am in love with him. There is nothing you or your racist friends can do about it."

Bo replied, "That is what you think. I am going to kill your gravel belly boyfriend. How could you shame our family like that? You disgust me! You know what, I forbid you from seeing him."

"I do not care what you say, Dad," Lisa said. "I will not give up on him for you or Mom. I love you both, but I love Edward too. I will not stop seeing him. I am old enough to choose who I should be with. You cannot control my life forever, Dad. You only hate him because he is Hispanic."

Bo said, "That's right I hate him. I would not let my daughter date no black, Hispanic, or Chinese man."

"I think it is time you get past your racism," Lisa screamed. "Let those people live their lives just as you are living yours," she continued softly. She turned to face him with tears streaming down her face. She said, "Ever since I was a little girl, you tried so hard to teach me to hate. I did not have any choice so I pretended to be racist. I am no longer a kid anymore, and I know what is right from wrong. I believe in equal opportunities for all. All you racist people can go to hades!"

Bo stormed out of the house in search of Lisa's boyfriend. He spent almost two hours searching for him. Finally, he gave up the search and returned home to call one of his buddies. Lisa left a couple of minutes after her dad stormed out. She went directly to Edward's house. She went there to let him know that her father knew about the relationship and was now looking for him. She wanted him to be careful because her father had promised to kill him. She felt that if anything happened to him, she would kill herself.

Edward said to her, "Do not worry, sweetheart. Nothing will happen to me." He began laughing.

Lisa shouted, "It is not funny! This is your life I am talking about. He has probably already called his friend by now. These people are very violent."

"Listen to me, baby," Edward interrupted. "You want me to stay home and hide from your dad and his friends. I cannot do that. If they come to my house and try to hurt me, I have to defend myself. Besides, your dad is probably trying to scare you so you will end the relationship." He paused and glared deep in her eyes and continued, "I will not give up on us. I love you, Lisa, so don't let your dad win."

Lisa replied in tears, "Sorry, honey. I love you with all my heart. If I have to sacrifice the love I have for you in order to save your life, then that's what I'll do. I have to break up with you. I do not want my dad to hurt you."

"Do you hear yourself?" Edward yelled, "You have no faith in us at all. Your father did not put me on this earth, and he cannot be the one to take me away from it. Have faith, my darling, because we are clearly meant to be together."

"You are so wise," Lisa replied. She looked down to the ground and said, "I have to go home now. I will see you tomorrow. If anything happens, please call the police." As she stepped out the door, she stopped and walked back and said, "I do not want to go home. I am so afraid for you." She ran to him and kissed Edward goodbye to remind him that she loves him.

Unfortunately for Edward and Lisa, Lisa's father did call one of his friends. He called Jack Wallace. He explained everything over the phone. Bo said, "Tonight we are going to kill that Hispanic. We need to get our town back from those Jews, blacks, and Hispanics. We have enough of them. Our children are getting exposed to them. They are all over the place. We are not moving out of our neighborhood for them. We will make it hard for them, and they will think twice before they move to our neighborhood."

Jack replied, "We need to gather at the house and have a meeting. We need a good solid plan." Jack was the mastermind of the bunch. So he called about fifteen of his friends to form a group to trash their non-white neighbors' homes and kill Edward. His first target was Willie Williams. He wanted to pay him a visit because his black son insulted his kid. And then they were going to kill that Hispanic boy for being involved with Bo's daughter.

As he was saying this, one of his friends, Earl Warren, stood up to him. Earl yelled, "I will not be a part of killing people! Listen to yourself! You are talking about killing people for stupid reasons. Do you think what you are going to do is right? We all have children and wives. What will happen to them if we go to jail for this? This is the time to stop the insanity. You guys sit around this table like disciples, as if you are planning good things, but you are not. You are trying to kill someone just because of the color of his skin. He is a human being." With a deep exasperation, he continued, "That's all I have to say to you guys."

All the men at the table were surprised to hear what Earl had just said. They wondered why he had a change of heart all of a sudden. In response to their faces of awe, he said, "I know in my heart what we are doing is wrong. Maybe it is a sign from God."

Jack replied, "Do not worry, Earl. We are going to heaven. God created us and loves us. We are his people and have the same color as God. He did not create those people. I have no clue where they came from, but he did not create them."

Earl said, "Jack, what makes you think God did not create every single human being who is living on this earth? How stupid could you be? I feel so sorry for your soul. I do not care if we are white; it does not mean anything, and it does not matter. This is about being humane and being able to get along with each other."

No one was listening to Earl. They did not change their minds. They decided to go along with their plan. They told Earl to shut up or get out. They felt as if he was not one of them, so he needed to leave and keep his mouth shut. They told him if he told anything to anyone, they would come after him. Earl got up, opened the door, and said, "I know I will have to answer to God one day, but for now, I am asking him to forgive me for my sins and my hatred I committed toward other people. God is watching you all, and may he have mercy on your souls."

The plan was set up as soon as Earl left, but he did not know when the assault would happen. Sunday night would be a weekend, and everybody would be home. Earl was afraid for himself and his family. He got the courage to go to the police station to report what Jack and his friends were planning to do. Although he went there, the police did not pay any attention to him because they thought he was lying.

10

Jeff Is Leaving for College

Jeff was leaving for college, and what a sad thing it was for his mom. "I have to go," he told his mother. "Be strong," he told his brother. "Goodbye," he told his father. He knew how his father was and decided to give him some advice. He said, "I pray to God that you change your ways toward other race. Well, Dad, you have a beautiful wife and two good sons. Enjoy it now and be open-minded toward other races, please. Do it for us. I love you, and keep in touch." He said he would write and call them. He gave his father a hug, then his mother, and then his brother. He got in his car and left for school.

He got himself situated in school, got to know his roommate, and adjusted well.

A few months later, he met a special person. One day on campus, Jeff was sitting outside under a tree, studying. He saw a beautiful black girl pass by him. He could not believe his eyes. He got up and closed his book. He started following her. He got too close, and she seemed startled. "Hi!" Jeff introduced himself. "My name is Jeff Wallace, and I'm a new student here." He asked for her name, but she refused to answer him.

She replied, "Why? Who are you, and why are you asking me for my name? Shouldn't you be asking some white girl for her name?"

Jeff said, "But I'm asking you for your name. Is anything wrong with that?"

She replied, "No! Not at all." She was irritated by his persistence and told him her name. "My name is Shela Berry, and I am a freshman too."

He responded with satisfaction, "Nice to meet you, Shela Berry. I hope we will see more of each other on campus."

She replied, "Shouldn't you be afraid to be seen around me? A black girl around a white boy. What will your friends say? Besides, you should not keep your hopes up."

"I want to see you more often," he said. "I want to get to know you better. I want to know what you like and what you do not like. I want to carry your books."

She answered, "I understand all that. It's what boys do. When you guys meet a girl, you will do anything to sleep with her."

He laughed and then said, "You have the wrong guy. You don't even know me that well, and you're already judging me. You know what, I forgive you. You don't know what you're saying. Anyway, are you seeing anyone?"

Shela responded, "No, I don't have a boyfriend. I don't need one, and I am not planning to have one. Well, at least not now. Do me a favor and forget you saw me, and go on and chase another woman. I came to college to learn and get a degree."

Jeff retorted, "Can we at least be friends? You're acting as if I asked you to marry me. I'd just like to know you first as friends."

They decided to meet up at the football field after her class. Jeff thought Shela was going to stand him up.

"I thought about it, but I changed my mind," Shela said.

Jeff replied, "Well, I'm glad you came."

He began by asking her general questions, such as what her major was, her age, and where was she from. Shela was twenty years old and wanted to be a scientist. She was from Mayberry. She asked him the same questions, and he told her that he wanted to be a brain surgeon, he was twenty years old, and he was from Kangroose.

He wanted to know more. "Enough about school. Would you like to go out on a date with me? I am a great cook. What is your favorite food?"

She laughed and replied, "I don't have a favorite food, but I will go to dinner with you. Do you really know how to cook?"

Jeff laughed. "No, not really. But how do you feel about Chinese food?"

She laughed harder and replied, "I love Chinese food!"

"So do I! Well, it's a date, and Chinese food it is! I will pick you up at eight. Now, can I walk with you back to class?" Jeff asked.

They started walking with each other.

After a couple of weeks of Jeff charming Shela and being the gentleman, he made Shela fall in love with him. Shela still had one concern. She hoped the relationship would work out, but she knew the race issue in the community might a problem. People would remind them every day of the interracial relationship and make racist remarks. She was not sure if she or Jeff were ready for that.

As he walked her to her dorm one night, the stars were glistening above their heads, with a big yellowish-white full moon that looked as if you could pick it out of the sky. He gazed deep into her eyes, held her by her face, and said, "Baby, I am ready for anything that comes our way. I love you and not them." That's when he planted the most romantic kiss the two of them had ever had.

A month had gone by. Shela and Jeff were invited to a party on the campus by a friend. On a Saturday night, Jeff picked up Shela and went to the party. They had a good time with each other until a man named David came. He was the son of a Jewish man and lived in the same town as Jeff. His family name was Wasserman. David remembered how racist Jack's father was and was still angry at Jack for the way he fired his father from the factory and how he treated his family. David walked over to Jeff and shouted drunkenly, "What are you doin' here, you racist pig?"

Confused, Jeff responded, "Excuse me? Do I know you? And why are you bothering us?"

In the middle of everyone at the party, he yelled, "Everyone, look. Meet Jeff. Jeff is the son of a man named Jack Wallace. Now that man, his daddy, is the most racist man in Greenleaf. His daddy will do anything to drive the other families out of the town if their skin color is different from his. He hates blacks, Jews, Hispanics, and Asians." He turned to Shela and asked her, "How do you feel about dating a racist man's son? Do you think his family will possibly accept you, a black girl, as a daughter-in-law?" He laughed obnoxiously and continued, "Think again! His daddy would probably kill himself before he accepted you." He turned around to the crowd and said, "You see old boy here! He is just like his father."

Shela turned to Jeff. "Tell me this is not true. Please!"

Jeff just stood up and did not have a word to say to Shela. He turned and punched David in the face. They started fighting with each other. The other students broke up the fight. Jeff wiped tears from his eyes and said in rage, "I am nothing like my father. You know my father and not me." Shela ran out of the room, crying, and Jeff ran after her, yelling after her to stop running so he could explain himself. She stopped and stared at Jeff with tears streaming down her face. She wanted to know why he did not tell her. Jeff wanted to tell her but only when the time was right. He did not want anything to ruin his chances of being with her nor did he want his father's ways to stop her from loving him. In all, he did not want her to judge him because of his father. He agreed that his dad was racist, but he was nothing like him. He did not want her to break up with him because of his father.

Shela wanted to know when he was going to tell his family about her. She said, "The woman you are in love with is black. How do you plan on explaining it to them?" She turned away from him and continued, "Well, never mind. Maybe you were going to hide me from them."

Jeff responded, "No, I was not thinking of hiding you. I love you too much. Listen, Shela! I am not proud of how my father is. I am actually ashamed of it. But my mother, my youngest brother, and I are the complete opposite of that man. I really hope you can try to understand why I kept this from you."

Shela just wanted Jeff to be truthful with her. Based on the way he looked at her and talked to her, she knew he was not racist. She became curious. She asked Jeff when he planned to tell his mother about her. Jeff responded, "Do not worry, sweetheart. I will tell her very soon."

Shela insisted, "I know you will need more time to tell your father about me, but I want to meet your mom and your little brother. Then you will meet my parents."

That same night, Jeff was expecting a phone call from his mother, and he planned to tell her everything about Shela and plan a time for them to meet.

A couple of hours later, Jeff received a phone call from his mother. He began the conversation by telling her about Shela. He told her that he had met a wonderful, beautiful woman that he was in love with. Then he mentioned that she was black. She took a minute before she could respond to Jeff's news. She replied, "I am sorry, son, that it took me a while to respond. I am happy for you." She stopped and stammered, "But what about Dad."

Jeff said to his mother, "What about Dad? He has his life, and I have mine. I am not goin' to let him choose who I should love. If he does not like me being with a black woman then that's too bad. Anyway, Mom, I want to know how you feel about me being in a relationship."

She replied, "Son, you know I will never come between two people falling in love. I would like to meet her. If you are happy, then so am I."

Jeff said, "Thank you, Mom. I love you, and I will talk to you next weekend. Say hello to Sam for me."

Jeff was so excited; he picked up the phone and called Shela to let her know he spoke to his mother about her and that he was ready to work on his dad. It would be hard for his father to change his mind. Jeff hoped to walk up to his father one day to find that his dad had become a different person and not racist. Jeff told Shela that his mom would be pleased to meet her. Shela replied to Jeff, "Do not worry. We can't change our parents. The only thing we can do is be their kids."

Jeff laughed. "It would take a miracle for him to change his lifestyle. Do not get me wrong: I love my dad, but I just don't like his perception of other people. Well, enough talking about my dad. Did you study for your test? If you need help, I'd be glad to help."

"Let's go to the library later on," Shela said.

"It's a date," Jeff responded. "See you later."

11

Jack and Caroline's
Twenty-Third Anniversary

Jack and his wife were about to celebrate their twenty-third anniversary. He made arrangements for a caterer and a host that would be hosting a party that they were planning to have. They started to send out the invitations to their family members and friends. He called his son Jeff to come from college for their party as well. He said he would come down for the party and would be bringing his girlfriend. Jack did not want to hear that because he did not like the idea of his son dating. Jack said he did not know that he had a girlfriend, and Jack insisted that they would love her. He wanted to know more about her. Jeff told her that she came from a nice family and that her name was Shela. With no hesitation, his dad reiterated for him to bring her to the party and that he would not take no for an answer.

As soon as they hung up, he called Shela. He begged her to attend his parents' anniversary party with him. She agreed to go with him. But she had some concerns. She said hesitantly said, "But, Jeff, you never introduced me to your father, and I doubt he knows I am black. So do you think this is the best way to meet your parents?"

Jeff replied, "You spoke with my mom over the phone. She knows all about you."

Shela answered, "Yes, but your dad doesn't know anything about me. How will he react when he sees me walking in and holding your hand in his house?"

Jeff made sure she knew that he would protect her, and if his father made a scene, then he would leave the party.

That brightened Shela's day, and she became excited about meeting her boyfriend's family in such a beautiful celebration. She went to her best friend's room to tell her and to ask her to go shopping with her for something to wear for the party. Her best friend was asking so many questions, and one of the main questions was if she were sure she wanted to go. She clarified how sure she was and how Jeff reassured her that he would take care of her. She believed in him. After hearing that, her friend shouted, "Let's go shopping, girl!"

They ventured off to the mall and went inside a boutique. They found a beautiful black dress with spaghetti straps. Shela went to the fitting room and tried on the dress. She loved it, and so did her friend. She found a nice pair of shoes to go with the glamorous dress. She got her hair and nails done, and before Shela and her friend could make it back to the dorms, they went out for lunch.

They began talking about Shela's main concerns about seeing the family. She mentioned, "I am not afraid of his dad, but I am afraid of the humiliation he may put me through. How can someone like Jeff's father be so ignorant? I mean, really, what does love have to do with the color of one's skin? I am a beautiful, intelligent black woman who comes from a nice family. My dad is a doctor, and my mother is a lawyer. I love myself and my race, but because of my race, I can't be with the man I love in peace."

Her friend said to Shela, "If you feel that way then why are you going to the party? Just don't go."

Shela replied, "No. I am going to have to make a stand for what I believe in. It takes one of us to make a difference, and I will meet them with my head on my shoulders. Don't worry about me. I will be fine. I am a strong woman."

The two of them then left the mall to get ready. Jeff would be picking her up to get on the road for the four-hour drive from the college to his house.

Jeff and Shela were having a great time as they drove to Jeff's home. They were laughing and talking about things that happened at school. Soon after, they arrived to Jeff's parents' home, where they bathed and got dressed. Jeff's father wasn't there when they arrived. The party was going to start at 7:00 p.m. Jeff asked Shela if she was okay before they left his room and headed into the party, where everyone else was. She assured him that she was ready with a kiss to his cheek. He held her hand, took a deep breath, and walked into the party. They walked down the empty hallway that led to the grand doors that opened to where everyone was in the party.

They walked in, and it felt like they were the stars of the show: everyone was looking at them. They heard a couple of gasps and many whispers. Soon this filled up the room. Many appeared shocked whereas others seemed upset. There were two people who stood out in the crowd, the only two people who seemed happy for Jeff. Jeff's mother and brother walked over to Jeff and gave him a huge hug. They then went over to Shela and hugged her as well. They took the two of them over to where the food was with glee and began talking. They asked Jeff about everything and even asked Shela about herself. They wanted to know where she was from, how her life was growing up, what she wanted to major in, and why she decided to attend their university.

Finally, tired of so many questions, Jeff walked away to get drinks for him and Shela. He saw his father standing at the edge of the punch table and decided to go get Shela. As he was approaching his father near the punch table, his father walked away from him. He called out to his father, waving and smiling. Jack just looked back, scolded him, and kept walking away.

Jack ran into Caroline, and Caroline realized what he was doing. She said, "Jack! Do not embarrass those kids. Go meet your son and his girlfriend. If you do not stop acting like this, you will lose your son through your hatred. Besides, if you want to act like this, at least do it when the guests are gone."

Jeff was behind his father while his mom was speaking to Jack. Jeff said, "Never mind, Mom. Shela and I will enjoy ourselves with you and Sam. I am through with speaking to Dad. It is your anniversary, Mom, so let's dance." He took his mom's hand and began dancing. When they were done, he grabbed Shela and danced with her as well. As everyone saw this, they began whispering to one another.

Jack was nowhere to be found. He was so upset and angry seeing his son with a black girl. Jeff and Shela had planned to stay over after the party instead of heading back to the school. After seeing how his father acted, he changed his mind. Jeff and Shela said their goodbyes to Jeff's mom and brother, and then they headed back to the college.

Jack waited until they left to come back to the house. He asked for Jeff, and Caroline told him that they left. She was angry at him for his behavior at the party. She expressed her feelings to Jack. While enraged, Jack said, "I am going back to the college to get Jeff out. I don't care if he likes it or not. My son should not associate with those people. He needs to go to an all-white-race school."

Caroline replied, "See, your father made you the way you are: all hateful. You can't make my two boys like you."

He responded, "Yes, I can. They are my boys too."

Caroline screamed, "Can't you see that our sons don't want to follow your hateful ways? You need to leave them alone and let them live their lives. Stop controlling them. They are great kids and we were blessed by God with them. We should be grateful that they didn't come out like you and your father."

He refuted, "My father raised me to be a great man, and I will raise my sons the same way."

In disagreement, Caroline replied, "Thank God Sam is following in his brother's footsteps and not yours."

Jack disregarded what his wife said to him and went upstairs to pack his handbag for tomorrow's drive down to his son's college. No matter what Caroline said to him, he would not listen to her. He said to Caroline, "This is my son, and I'll raise him the way I want. Neither you nor anyone else will stop me."

Caroline replied, "They are my sons too, Jack. Remember that. You can never change Jeff's mind. He is in love."

Jack responded, "Not with that black girl."

Caroline refuted, "So what if he fell in love with a black woman? Black or white, we are all the same in God's eyes. Go get Jeff and make a fool out of yourself."

Jack replied, "And I will." Then he stormed off.

The next day, Jack got up at six in the morning, got his handbag and his keys, and left. He stopped at the gas station to fill up his gas tank and bought a couple of snacks for the long drive. On his way back to the car, he decided to call his wife to let her know that he was on his way. Caroline said to him, "I was praying for you last night. I prayed you'd change your mind." Jack immediately hung up the phone. Caroline shouted through the receiver, "You are a mad man!" and hung up.

He got in his car and drove like a mad man, just as his wife had called him. Two miles away from home, he got into a car accident. A local family saw the accident and called the police. When the ambulance arrived at the scene, he was unresponsive. He was badly hurt, so the paramedic put him in the ambulance and took him to the nearest hospital. Jack was in a coma, and they decided to transfer him to his town's hospital so his wife and son could be by his side. She asked her son to call Jeff to inform him of what had just happened to his father.

That Monday morning, Jeff was on his way to class when he got the call from his little brother. Sam told him that their dad was in an accident and was now in the hospital. Jeff wondered how it had happened, but Sam told him that he needed to come as soon as possible. Jeff hung up the phone and rushed to the school office and told them the news. He received a pass of grievance for a few days. He called Shela before he left and told her that he had to go home as soon as possible. Shela said to Jeff, "Wait, I'm going with you. I will get myself a pass."

Jeff and Shela left for Greenleaf that night. When they arrived, they went straight to the hospital. Jeff asked a nurse for his dad's room number. The room number was room 200. When he arrived, he found his mother sitting on a chair at the foot of her father's bed. He walked up to her and gave her a hug and then a kiss on the forehead. He then walked to his father on the bed and stood beside him, staring into his shut eyes. He kissed him on the forehead. Jeff began talking to him. He bent over and whispered in his ear, "I love you."

Shela touched Jeff on his arm and said, "I am sorry about your dad, sweetheart."

The next morning, Caroline went home to get a few things to bring back to the hospital. As Caroline and Sam were leaving their home,

Officer Kelly, Detective Kate, and two other officers arrived with the warrant in hand for Jack's arrest. Detective Kate recognized that Caroline had been crying, so she asked her if everything was all right. That was when Caroline told her about what had happened to Jack.

Caroline responded to Detective Kate while mourning. "Jack was on his way to our son's school, and he got into a bad car accident, leaving him in a coma."

Detective Kate turned to Officer Kelly and said, "I kind of feel sorry for that racist guy!"

He responded, "If we did not feel sorry than we would be inhumane."

Since Jack was in a coma, Detective Kate placed a twenty-four-hour guard to by his room until he awakened—if he ever woke up.

12

The Angel

Jack Wallace had been in a coma for a week now, and there was nothing the doctor could do but wait. One night, Jack had a visit from an angel.

The angel said to him, "Jack! Jack! Wake up." Jack tried to open his eyes to see who was calling him. His eyes hardly opened to see the angel's face. The only thing he could see was a shiny light, and he could barely talk.

He said, "Who's there?" He saw a man with a white robe on. Jack stood up by the side of his bed and found the strength to talk.

He questioned the angel, "Who are you?" However, the angel did not answer. Jack asked the question again and wanted to know why he was there.

The angel turned to him and replied, "I am here because you called me."

Jack replied, "I did not call anybody."

The angel replied, "You did call for help."

Jack asked, "Where am I?"

The angel responded, "You are in the hospital. You were involved in a horrible accident and are now in a coma."

In awe, Jack pondered how and why he was in the hospital, and how he could he possibly be speaking to this person talking to him while he was in a coma.

The angel continued, "You are the only one who can see and speak to me."

"Where is my wife? Can she hear or see me? My eyes are open. Can she see that?" Jack shouted.

The angel walked closer to Jack and stared deep into his eyes. He answered, "No. She sits next to you. She sees you laying on this bed in a coma." The angel turned away from him and continued, "What a wonderful wife you have. She sits at your bedside, praying and hoping to hear you and see you awake." He then faced him again and let Jack know that he was his angel sent down to earth by God for him. "He sent me to bring you to see him."

Jack began to sob and say, "Why me? What did I do for him to see me?"

"I cannot answer that," the angel replied, "He is the only one who holds the answer to that question, not me. I am only his messenger, Jack."

Jack said, "But you said you are my angel; you must know something." And with a deep exasperation, Jack continued, "Well, can I at least see your face?"

The angel pulled back his white veil. He stared at Jack and said, "Do you believe that angels exist?"

In disbelief, Jack said he did not. Jack said to the angel, "You are black; I never knew angels could be black. I thought there were only white angels."

The angel whispered, "You seem surprised. Were you expecting a white angel?"

After hearing Jack's response to the color of his skin, the angel informed him that God was not racist. The angel began to glow and change colors to show Jack that they were all God's children. The angel said, "So judge me not based on the color of my skin."

Jack responded to the angel, "You can change the color of your skin." The angel stretched out his arms and nodded.

The angel let Jack know that God created different races for his own purpose: the purpose of seeing whether we could live amongst one another, since he loves all of us. In the end, every single human being must answer to God. "God does not pick sides. He just wants a clean heart, with no hate. He wants you to feed your brother and your sister when they are hungry, clothe them when they do not have any clothes, shelter them when they need a place to sleep, help them when they cry for help, and always be good to each other. He wants all of us to love and follow him as one. That is all he wants and all he asks for."

Jack asked the angel again, "What does God want from me?"

The angel replied, "It is for you to ask him. Come, it is time to go."

The angel held Jack's hand and went up with him. Jack turned around and saw his body laying down on a hospital bed helplessly, with his wife holding his hand, praying for him. He shouted, "Caroline! Caroline! I am here, honey. Tell my kids I love them." He faced the angel and continued, "I cannot believe I am dead. I have a family to take care of." Together, Jack and the angel vanished and appeared in a huge place with a bright light and fumes. Jack could not see anything, and the angel left him. Jack said, "What is this place? Please tell me where am I."

Finally, he squinted and saw three men far away from him, waiting for him. When Jack approached the three men, he said hello to them. He wanted to know where he was. None of them responded to Jack's question. The three men then said, "We are the servants of God. He tells us what to do and who to look after down on earth." The third angel continued, "We have been expecting you, Mr. Wallace. Do you know why you are here?"

Jack answered, "No, I don't." And then he looked around, feeling tiny compared to the size of the atmosphere, and continued, "Why is it so hot in here? Am I close to hades?"

The third angel replied, "No, Mr. Wallace. God has to judge you first. He tells whether you deserve to go to heaven or hades." He paused for moment and continued, "Mr. Wallace, your test will begin." Jack saw a couple of doors that were painted different colors and wondered what was behind those doors. One of the angels answered, "Each of these doors contains your fate. You are here to see your fate and destiny."

"I don't understand," Jack said.

The third angel replied, "Of course you do not. You have been so occupied with yourself and your hatred for other races that you forgot God even existed. You kept persecuting his children. I do not even think you remember the last time you called upon God for someone else other than yourself." He then asked Jack to choose a door. He accepted and chose a white one. The door opened as Jack watched in fear. He then thought of the angel who brought him there and asked the angels of his whereabouts. He wanted to speak to that angel.

The second angel questioned, "The black angel?"

Jack replied, "Yes!"

The first angel chuckled and replied, "Mr. Wallace, you are white. Why would you want to know the black angel's whereabouts? You spent half of your life hating and fighting other races. You should not have a black angel. You are white, remember?"

"But my angel is black," Jack stammered.

The second angel said, "Yes! Yes, he is."

Jack whispered, "He is nicer then you three white angels."

The first angel questioned, "How many people did you know whose color or race was different from your own? Did you give yourself a chance to know whether they were kind or not?"

The second angel then turned to him and continued, "You just hate all of them. You do not take time to know anyone who is not white."

Jack shouted, "You are not bein' fair to me."

The first angel said, "Let's talk about fair, Mr. Wallace. How fair were you with others on earth?"

Jack answered, "You call yourself servants of God. Why didn't ya give me a sign of what I was doing wrong or where I was going wrong?"

The first angel whispered, "We did, Mr. Wallace. You chose to ignore it."

The second angel continued, "Earl spoke the word of God, and you did not even take a moment to understand him. He was like you. He came to the meeting to listen to you make plan about hurting innocent people. Then all of a sudden, he had a change of heart."

The third angel continued, "Who do you think changed Earl's heart?"

The first angel answered, "God did. This was all because he asked God for forgiveness. He wanted to change his life."

The second angel stepped up and continued, "He did not want part of your hatred. The words he spoke were God's words."

The first angel continued, "You must have thought he betrayed you or he was crazy, but no, Jack. He came as one of God's prophets." As we walked over to the double doors, he said, "Now, Mr. Wallace, I want you to open the door."

Anxiously, Jack walked toward the white door, reached over, turned the knob, and opened it.

The first angel said to him, "Are you sure this is the door you want to open to find salvation?"

Jack answered, "Everything that is white is pure."

The second angel shook his head and said, "You do not get it, Mr. Wallace. You are here to find truth, and you are still blinded by your terrible ways." Jack opened the white door, took two steps, and leaped down. From there, he was stuck in a dark place and screamed for help. He screamed, "Get me out of here! There is someone here. Who are these people? They are reaching for me, and I do not want to be here."

The angel said, "They are just like you, Mr. Wallace. These are people who defied against our father. They are here to answer to God. They too had their second chance to change their ways and to follow God."

One of the angels grabbed Jack by the hand and helped him get out of that place. "Let's try another door, Mr. Wallace, and see what is behind it," the angel said. When Jack opened the next door, he saw a glimpse of his past on earth. He saw all of the wrong he had done to others all his life. While reliving those awful moments, Jack started to weep in disappointment of his actions. He felt really terrible.

Jack fell down to his knees and said, "I do not have any excuse for the way I treated others in my past. Please forgive me, God, for my sins and for being racist. I want to be a changed man. I was wrong for judging other for the color of their skin. I want to repent my soul to my Lord, Jesus Christ. I hurt my family, and I preached hate around as if I were preaching the gospel. My heart is open to receive the truth, God."

The angel said, "Mr. Wallace, God hears your words and knows what is taking place in your heart right now. He loves all his children, even when they are wrong. Open your heart and your soul to let him in, call him when you need him, and ask when you're in need. Now, Mr. Wallace, you have to open the last door, but you won't be able to get out of this door."

For some odd reason, Jack wasn't too afraid to open the last door. He felt God's presence with him. Jack immediately opened the last door and walked in.

13

Jack Wakes up from His Coma

Caroline was at the hospital, sitting next to Jack and praying that he would wake up. No matter how stressed and worried she was, she continued to hold on to her faith, believing Jack would soon awaken from the coma.

"Lord, give me comfort during this time of distress. I know you are an amazing God and can do all things. I believe that you are here and you are healing my husband. Please, Lord, let him wake up and be completely healed. I thank you and give you all of the praise, in Jesus's name. Amen!"

Suddenly, Jack woke up from the coma. He opened his eyes and saw his wife sitting by his side. He said, "Hey," to his wife, and she jumped out of the chair.

"You are awake! You came back to me, Jack."

Jack asked his wife, "What day and time is it, Caroline?"

"Today is Sunday the seventh," she responded.

"You are talking, Jack, I am very happy to hear your voice." She called for the nurse, and the nurse came and stood in awe. Immediately, the nurse called the doctor to give him the update on Jack.

Jack told Caroline that he had to get out of the hospital immediately. "I have a mission to accomplish." Caroline stared at him in confusion and wondered what Jack was talking about.

Caroline said, "You just woke up out of a coma. You need to take things slow and wait until the doctor clears you and says everything is okay."

"I am talking about saving people's lives," Jack replied. "You will not understand now, but I will explain it all to you later. I have to stop them." Jack got up from his hospital bed and started to sneak out of his room. The officer who was there to watch him was busy talking on the phone and didn't notice Jack sneaking out the room. He started running down the hallway with his hospital gown still on. He was very tired, but he didn't care, and he kept on running. People tried to stop him, but he was too quick and full of determination.

The doctor shouted at Jack, "You need to stop. You are not cleared to leave. There are some test that need to be done."

"I feel *fine!* God has healed me." Jack did not turn around to see who was after him. He finally made it out of the hospital and continued on to complete his mission.

His wife was driving around the city, looking for him. When she found him, she told him to get in the car. "Let's go back to the hospital," she demanded.

Jack replied, "No! I do not want to go back to the hospital. I'm fine, Caroline. Just relax and trust me. I know what I'm doing. God is on my side, and he gave me another chance to live a righteous life. You are my wife. Just trust me and let me do what I have to do. Honey, take me to Leaf Street. It is very important that I get there as soon as possible."

Caroline said, "What's going on Jack?"

He responded, "I have to stop a group of friends of mine from killing innocent people. They are going to kill a Hispanic boy and a black boy. I have to stop them. I am a new man, a man of God. I have to convince my fellow brothers to see the same light that I have seen." Caroline believed Jack and took him to Leaf Street as he asked. When they arrived, they saw a group of people coming down to the street, singing and yelling racial slurs.

They were carrying guns, baseball bats, and steel rods in their hands as they marched furiously toward Leaf Street. As they approached both Willie and Edward's homes, they stopped and commanded them to come out. As they continued to call them out, Willie and his family stayed in their house, terrified of what might happen. Edward stayed hidden in his home.

"Come out! You, black and Latino, are going to die today. We are taking back our neighborhood. Come out or we're going to burn your houses down."

Willie said to his family that he was going to go outside to make them go away. He told his family to stay inside and ordered his son Martin not to come out for any reason. As Willie opened the door to step outside, the angry mob got more violent and started to approach him. Edward saw what was happening through his window and felt he had to do something to help Willie. Immediately, Edward came out his house to assist Willie against the angry mob.

As the mob got closer and ready to kill Edward and Willie, Jack started running toward them, screaming, "*Stop!*" Bo, Jack's friend, heard someone screaming and turned toward the direction it was coming from. He saw Jack in his hospital gown, running toward them.

"Hey, guys! Look, its Jack!" At first, Bo and everyone who was with him to kill Willie and Edward started cheering with joy to see Jack. They thought Jack had come from the hospital to help kill Willie, Martin, and Edward.

But as Jack got closer to the crowd, they heard him scream, "No! Stop! Put your weapons down!"

In confusion, Bo said to Jack, "Are you crazy? What are you talking about? We are here to end this madness that these non-white folks are bringing into our neighborhood."

Jack replied, "I am here to end this madness as well. I am here to end the violence that we bring to our black, Hispanic, Jewish, and non-white brothers and sisters.

"Do you hear yourself? You must still be under the influence of the hospital drugs or going nuts from the coma you just got out of," said Bo.

"I'm not on any drugs, nor am I going crazy," Jack replied to Bo. "Everyone, please listen to me. I have something to say to you all, and it needs to be heard today." The mob immediately stopped and looked at Jack fiercely as if they wanted to shut him up and go on killing both Edward and Willie. As Jack finally got their attention, he started to tell them what God wanted him to say. "I was in a coma, and then I died. When I died, I found out it wasn't the end of all things, but it was the just the beginning. Now everyone knows me as one of the most racist and hatful people toward other races in the town of Greenleaf. I am now a changed man since I woke up out of this coma. I died a hateful, angry, selfish, racist, and an unrighteous man blinded by his own sins. God gave me another chance. I am now reborn a man blessed by God with a chance to live a new life. I have seen the truth and have been sent back by God to reveal the truth to you all and everyone I can reach. The devil has blinded us with many sinful natures that we cover ourselves with, which blinds us from seeing the light of God. The god we believe in, who accept us hating other races, is not the true living God. It is a god we created. The god that we created does not live, but the God that lives wants to live in you. While in my coma, a black angel was assigned to me. I was afraid, not knowing what was going to happen, but as my spirit left my body, the angel said to me, 'Don't be afraid. Come! There is something that I have to show you.'

"The angel brought me into a place I had never seen before. Then I felt like I was going through a time portal. In this portal, I met other angels, and there were three doors there. Each door had its own purpose. The first door was a place of darkness that was completely absent of God's peace and presence. In the second door, the angel was showing a flashback of my life, from when I was a baby all the way to my present. He showed me my life and all I have done that wasn't in God's will for my life. I saw all the wrong I have done to others all my life, and I was convicted. God allowed me to feel his anger toward my wrongdoing to others and for the hatred I had toward different races. I thought the way I was living was good, but truly it was an abomination in God's eyes. The angel said that God made us all in his image. That means we all resemble who God is and looks like. If I hate people because of the color of their skin, their culture, or their race, then I hate God as well. That goes the same for you all in Greenleaf. You must love each other as God loves us all. We are all made from the same God, which make us all family.

"After the angel had revealed the truth to me, I felt a heavy burden on my heart because I had lived such an ungodly life and now I was dead. The angel looked at me and said, 'God has created two places: one for his children, and the other for those who stood against him and his ways … heaven and hades. It is time for you to be judged by the one true King.'

"Then the angel told me to open the last door, so I did and walked in. The place that I saw as I walked through the door was very beautiful and full of joy and peace. The color of this world was so vibrant that it made the color on earth look dull. The road was made of gold, and the people there were happy and seemed to be worry free. People of all races lived together peacefully next to each other and treated each other as family. Race did not exist here, only love. I asked the angel, 'What is this place?'

"He responded to me, 'This is the kingdom of God: heaven.' I couldn't believe my eyes. Then the angel continued, 'Mr. Wallace, this is where God's obedient children come when they die on earth.'

"Then I said to the angel, 'This place is so beautiful and so different than on earth. Everyone is happy; children are praying with each other. Everyone is walking hand in hand, no matter what race they are. They eat with each other with no violence or hate among them. I want to be among them. Tell me what to do to be part of that wonderful place. I do not want to go back to that dark place. I want to stay here.' We walked around for a while. I observed what was in heaven, but I knew that the angel was bringing me somewhere. We approached a huge golden palace with enormous white double doors. As we walked in, I found myself in a gigantic, bright-white room with a magnificent throne, and someone was sitting on it. Immediately, I knew that the person sitting on the throne was the great I Am. Though I wasn't near him, I felt his holy presence from a distance. I fell to my knees, knowing where I was destined to go, which was hades. I started to ask the angel, 'Is it too late for me to change? Is it too late for me to be saved?' The angel didn't say anything and just stared at me in complete silence. I screamed, 'God, please forgive me! Please give me another chance to do right!' I continued to cry and beg for forgiveness. The angel told me to stay and he would be back when it is time to be judged.

"Moments later, my angel came back and said that it was time to go. I said, 'I don't want to go to hades. I want to stay here in heaven. I was blind, and now I see. Please give me a chance to fix my wrongdoing and live for God.'

"The angel glanced at me and said, 'You are not going to hades. You are going back to earth. If you do not understand the gospel, then you will not understand God, our Father. You need a change of heart, Mr. Wallace. You were a prophet of hate, but you will become a prophet of love. God has given you a second chance. This is a chance to do good from now on, and he will be watching you. You will live with many races and treat them as your brothers and sisters. We will send you back to earth with a mission. Your mission is to stop your men from continuing the act of violence against those innocent people.'

"Then I asked the angel how God expects me to do that. 'They will not listen to me.'

"The angel said, 'This was your wrongdoing, so you have to undo your mistake. You will make them listen as you influenced them to listen before. You will speak the word of God to them. God does not want these people to get hurt or killed. Now you have the wisdom of God to stop those innocent people from being harmed.'

"I told him I would and then bowed my head down and said, 'Forgive me, oh Lord Jesus, for my hatred and racist ways against others in the past. I was not doing the right things. Please, God, have mercy on my family and me. I need your help, God. What do I say to those people? How do I make them listen to me? They will not believe me when I tell them I was here with your angels.'

"One of the angels responded, 'Have faith and they will believe you. You will convert them with God's words. Tell them what you have seen. Jack, listen to God's voice and speak what he places in your heart. The Holy Spirit will be with you.'

"I was really happy that God forgave me for the way I was in the past. That moment, I was ready to change the lives around me with the gospel of Jesus Christ. I asked the angel, 'When will I see our Father and you and the other angels again?' He said I would see them again when the time comes and the trumpet blasts from heaven. Jesus will hold me in his arms and say to me, 'Welcome home, my son.'

"'Mr. Wallace, it is time to go back home. Your family and neighbors are waiting for you. May God be with you! Enjoy your second chance in life.'

"That is when I woke up from my coma, blessed to be standing here today. God has given me another chance at life. I am here to bring truth and undo what I have created. I have a mission to stop the confusion in our lives about race and who is greater. God created us all to be equal and loves us all the same. We need to destroy the hatred in our hearts and the separation in our lives and community. We have to do it now before it is too late. You don't have to wait until you die and are headed for hades to decide that you want to change. You can change and live righteously now!"

As Jack finished talking, the mob seemed to calm down. "Go and ask for forgiveness, my brothers and sisters. Make amends with everyone you have offend and treated unjustly." Jack got off the car and approached Willie and said that he was sorry for all he had done against him and his family. He then approached Martin, who stood by the door of his house, and asked him to forgive him for beating him. As Jack was trying to make amends with Martin and his family, Detective Kate, Officer Kelly, and four other officers pulled up in front of the Williams' home.

"Jack, I am Detective Kate, and you are under arrest. You have the right to remain silent. Anything you say can and will be used against you in a court of law. You have the right to an attorney. If you cannot afford an attorney, one will be provided for you. Do you understand the rights I have just read to you? With these rights in mind, do you wish to speak to me?"

"No, I do not have anything to say, Detective," replied Jack. Officer Kelly came up to Jack, put him in handcuffs, put him in the police car, and left.

14

In Court

The next morning, Jack had to appear in court. He was offered a public attorney, but he refused. Many were shocked and questioned why he would decline a public attorney. His reason he gave them was that Jesus Christ would be his lawyer and he would bring justice in court. When he arrived at the courthouse, he saw the Robinson family, his family, and many other people who lived in his neighborhood. As the judge walked into the room, everyone began to settle down and waited to see what was going to happen next.

"All rise!"

"The Court of General Sessions, Twenty-Eighth Judicial Circuits, is now in session. The Honorable Judge Matthew E. Brown is presiding."

After having Martin and the other witnesses swear that they would be telling the truth and nothing but the truth, the trial begin. "We are here today to put Mr. Jack Wallace on trial for assault charges against Martin Williams as well as for attempting to inflict physical harm to other victims in his neighborhood by gathering a group of white people to beat on Edward and Mr. Robinson."

As the trial began, the judge called Martin to the bench. When he got up to walk toward the front, he walked straight toward the judge and stood there silently. "Martin, you have to sit on the bench," said Judge Brown. Martin stood in front of the judge for a few seconds and said something that shocked everyone there.

"I want to drop all charges against Jack Wallace."

The judge looked at Martin and said, "What do you mean, Martin?"

"I want to drop all charges against Mr. Wallace," Martin said again. Slowly, one by one, the other witnesses stood up and said they wanted to drop charges against Mr. Wallace. Judge Brown, the lawyers, Detective Kate, Officer Kelly, and other people in the courtroom were looking around the room with confusion. Martin continued, "Your Honor, something happened yesterday that lifted the anger out of my heart and put forgiveness into it. I forgive Mr. Wallace for his wrongdoing, and I don't want to press any charges against him." The rest of the witnesses and victims agreed on forgiving Jack Wallace. As this was happening, Jack sat in his chair with tears coming out of his eyes and falling down against his cheeks. Then the judge said to Martin and the other victims, "If you are not going to press charges against Mr. Wallace, then I have to dismiss all the charges. Mr. Wallace, you are free to go."

Mr. Wallace and his family embraced each other with love and tears of joy. This was truly a blessing and a miracle from God. When Detective Kate approached Martin, she asked him why he dropped the charges. Why did he have a change of heart? He told her that the man who beat him up and tried to harm other innocent people was not in the room. He said Mr. Wallace was a new man, and his old self was no more.

"How do you know that for sure, and how do you know that he isn't putting on an innocent act so that he won't go to jail and pay for what he did to you and others?"

Martin said, "God changes people, and Jack is one person who God placed on my heart who has been transformed into a new man. It was place in my heart to forgive him, so that is what I am going to do." The detective stood the speechless and nodded her head as she accepted what Martin was saying. She slowly walked away. The Williams and the Wallace family, along with everyone in the courtroom, left and went their separate ways, with peace in their hearts about what happened today in court.

That night, Jeff came to talk to his dad about something. "What did you want to talk to me about, son?" Jeff told his dad that he wanted to marry Shela. At first, Jeff thought that the father would be upset and against it, but he was up for a surprise. Jack told Jeff that he was happy for him and couldn't wait to learn more about his future wife. Jack also started to apologize to Jeff about how he had acted during the anniversary party. He made peace with and received forgiveness from his son, and things grew in their relationship from that day forward. Everything that happened that day changed a lot of people's hearts and views of God.

Jack's friend Bo started to change his ways and became accepting about his daughter Lisa's relationship with Edward. God had really touched and changed many lives in the town of Greenleaf that day.

Before Jack went to bed that night, he read his Bible. God was not done with him yet, and he realized this was just the beginning of his mission. To help him prepare and know what God wanted him to do, he had to read God's Word. As he was reading, he stopped at a scripture that truly reflected what happened to him that day in court.

"When you are on the way to court with your adversary, settle your differences quickly. Otherwise, your accuser may hand you over to the judge, who will hand you over to an officer, and you will be thrown into prison. And if that happens, you surely won't be free again until you have paid the last penny." (Matthew 5:25–26 NLT)

Printed in the United States
By Bookmasters